We're Moving!

To Max and Leo — A.G. and C.G.

For all the brave kids around the world, who had
to stay indoors during long quarantine days. — Z.Ö.

A STUDIO PRESS BOOK

First published in the UK in 2022 by Studio Press Books,
an imprint of Bonnier Books UK,
4th Floor, Victoria House, Bloomsbury Square, London WC1B 4DA
Owned by Bonnier Books,
Sveavägen 56, Stockholm, Sweden

www.bonnierbooks.co.uk

Text © 2022 Adam and Charlotte Guillain
Illustration © 2022 Zeynep Özatalay

1 3 5 7 9 10 8 6 4 2

ISBN 978-1-78741-942-1

MIX
Paper from
responsible sources
FSC® C104723
FSC
www.fsc.org

Edited by Frankie Jones and Sophie Blackman
Designed by Claire Munday
Production by Emma Kidd

A CIP catalogue for this book is available from the British Library
Printed and bound in China

We're Moving!

STUDIO PRESS

It's moving day! We've packed away.
We're loading up the van.
I'm taking one last look across
the city while I can.

The birds are on our balcony –
I feed them every day.
I wonder who'll look after them
when we have moved away.

Ever since I was a baby, we've lived
in our flat up high.
Now that we're moving far away,
it's time to say goodbye!

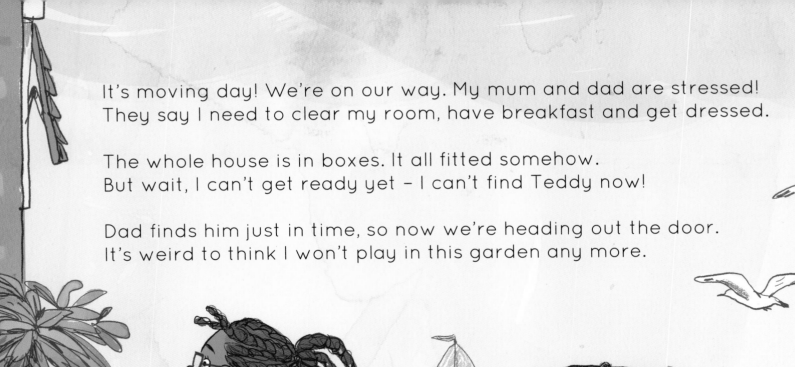

It's moving day! We're on our way. My mum and dad are stressed!
They say I need to clear my room, have breakfast and get dressed.

The whole house is in boxes. It all fitted somehow.
But wait, I can't get ready yet – I can't find Teddy now!

Dad finds him just in time, so now we're heading out the door.
It's weird to think I won't play in this garden any more.

It's moving day! It's not OK!
We just don't want to go.
We've got to leave behind the wall
we mark each time we grow.

We're moving to another country,
very far away.
What if there's no pizza there
or places we can play?

Our tummies feel all jumpy now –
we've got to leave our street.
The car is so jam-packed with stuff,
there's no room for our feet.

It's moving day! No time to play. We're heading somewhere new.
I'm feeling so excited that I don't know what to do!

I'm getting a new bedroom, and new friends and so much more.
Mum's taken out my suitcase and Dad's hoovering the floor.

The van is packed with all our stuff. There's nothing left behind.
Our new home's just a day away – I wonder what we'll find.

It's moving day! Hip-hip hooray! Our house is upside down.
We're going to a whole new home, new school and brand new town!

Will the new place have camels, elephants or baboons?
Will people get around in cars or travel in balloons?

I heard it snows there – maybe we'll all go to school on skis.
I guess I don't mind all that much, as long as they have cheese!

It's moving day! Yes, now – today! The moving men have come.
We've emptied all our cupboards and I've tried to help my mum.

We're moving nearer Granny, so we'll see her every day.
I'm trying not to mind my friends will be so far away.

My cat is in his basket and I think it's time to go.
I hope he doesn't mind we're going somewhere he won't know.

It's moving day! The sky is grey. We're clearing every room.
We've taken out the boxes and we've swept up with a broom.

Mum tells me, "There are mountains where we're going, wait and see!"
Don't giants live in mountains? Just how scary will it be?

My sister's looking worried as we go out to the car.
I tell her we can come back soon to visit – it's not far.

It's moving day! I want to play, but there's so much to do.
I've got to pack away my toys and find my missing shoe!

I'm going to miss these meadows where I walk the dog and play.
But Dad says where we're going we'll see new things every day.

We stop and have a hug and he says, "Hey, it will be great!"
I'm trying not to cry now as we shut the garden gate.

"It's moving day! Not snoozing day," calls Aly with a smile.
"Your dad has brought us into town, there's only one more mile."

I've always really loved it when we sit on deck like this.
The stories and the stargazing are things I'm going to miss.

I don't know how I feel about our new home, way up high.
But now the taxi's coming and Dad calls, "It's time to fly!"

It's moving day and come what may,
there is no turning back!
We're on our way to somewhere new,
and then we'll all unpack.

We call out, "Are we there yet?"
Oh, the journey seems so far.
We have a little snooze,
then someone calls out...

We moved today and it's OK.
The city lights are bright.
I miss the stars but Dad will still
tell stories every night.

I think about tomorrow and the
things that we can do,
and feel a little buzz because
we're starting something new.